Elaine Israel

CONTENTS

Weather or Not, It's Cold or Hot	3
Fungus and Green Slime	10
Behind the Big Screen	14
On the Smaller Screen	18
Even If the Head's Not in the Gutter, It's a Bad Break	22
That's the Spirit!	26
Take a Hoist to Top It Off	29
Index	32

Rigby

How many languages can *you* speak? When you finish reading this book, the answer may surprise you. This is a book about languages. Sort of. They aren't languages from other countries, though. These languages are known as *jargon*, or *lingo*. That's the vocabulary used by people in a particular profession or group when they speak among themselves. It's a shortcut way of saying things. And as you'll see, many of the words may mean one thing to the people who use them and another thing to the rest of us.

WEATHER OR NOT, IT'S COLD OR HOT

Most weather forecasters on TV and the radio speak clearly. They have to. They have to tell you whether the weather is hot or cold. They have to tell you if it's clear or raining. But how do weather people talk to each other? When forecasters speak of *lamb blasts* and *dog days*, the words have little to do with baas or barks.

Ever hear of these terms—**chase hotel** or **white elephant**? These are terms for a vehicle—often an old pickup truck or station wagon—that has been fixed up by storm chasers. Storm chasers are people who follow storms like tornadoes in order to study them.

If a weather reporter said to you that there's a **chocolatero** or **chocolate gale** coming, what do you think that might mean? He's saying that we're about to get some moderate to strong northern winds that bring dropping temperatures with them. They create the kind of day when a cup of hot chocolate tastes extra delicious.

Here's an expression that goes a little beyond "It's raining cats and dogs." The **dog days** of summer are yucky, humid days that come from mid-July to early September. Temperatures climb. Thunder rumbles. Some people believe that during this time dogs tend to become wilder. Not true. The term "dog days" probably comes from an ancient myth and has nothing to do with your pet dachshund. Like humans, dogs may simply be reacting to the extreme temperatures.

Dustbusting might be something you do when you clean under your bed; however, it means just the opposite when it comes to the weather. Dustbusting refers to the ways in which farmers keep topsoil from blowing away on very windy days—such as building fences and planting shrubs and trees that help hold down the soil. When *you* dustbust you're trying to get rid of the dirt, but farmers are trying to hold on to it!

In England and Scotland, **lamb blasts** are what weather forecasters call the snowstorms that are like our April snow showers. Lamb blasts usually happen in the spring when new lambs are born. Sheep farmers need to be kept up to date about these storms because they can be deadly to these cuddly newborn animals. And that would be BAAAAAD!

Got a **little brother** or **little sister**? Maybe, but I bet your siblings cause less trouble than these. Little brothers and little sisters are terms for smaller storms that sometimes follow big ones. Little brothers and little sisters often trail after their older siblings. Get it?

And you thought wind and fog was just wind and fog. Apparently not. Did you know that certain kinds of wind and fog make snow melt faster? Weather scientists call these kinds of wind and fog **snoweaters**. And speaking of fog, a **fogeater** is a strong airport beacon, a search light, or even a full moon. When their light passes through the fog, the light seems to eat the fog along its path. Want fries with that fog?

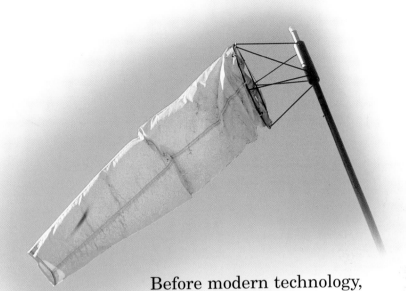

Before modern technology, airports often depended on a wind sock for weather information. A wind sock looks like a cloth funnel-shaped tube stuck on the top of a tall pole. The wind would fill the sock. Whichever way the sock blew, that was the direction of the wind. Sometimes, in really thick fog, the sock couldn't be seen. So the airport was **socked in**.

So . . .

Whether the weather is cold,

Whether the weather is hot,

We'll weather the weather

Whatever the weather,

Whether we like it or not.

FUNGUS AND GREEN SLIME

When I want a pizza, I don't like to wait. No one does. So the people behind the counter work fast. Who has time for long descriptions? That may be one reason why pizza lingo is short and to the point.

Take this little quiz and see if you can figure out what kind of pizza is being ordered each time.

1. One large pizza — **destroy it**

   a) nothing on it   **c)** everything on it

   b) 1/2 and 1/2   **d)** two cans of anchovies

The right answer is **c**.
When the server says, "Destroy it," it means a pizza with ALL the toppings on it.

2. A medium pizza with **flyers** and **fungus**

   a) black olives and green peppers

   b) pepperoni and mushrooms

   c) cheese and sausage

   d) bacon and pineapple

The right answer is **b.** A pepperoni slice is called a "flyer" because it looks like a Frisbee®. And a mushroom is a type of fungus, so . . . see how that works?

3. A small pizza, extra **green slime**

   a) green olives

   b) bacon

   c) spinach

   d) green peppers

The right answer is **d.** This is a term for green peppers, which get kind of mushy when they're not stored well. Yummy.

4. A medium pizza with **screamers**

   a) sausage pieces

   b) canned mushrooms

   c) black olives

   d) onions

The right answer is **b**.
Canned mushrooms sometimes
make high-pitched sounds when
they're rubbed on a hot surface.

So, whether you
like your screamers
canned or your
fungus fresh, if
your local pizza
joint serves it up,
it's got to be great!

13

BEHIND THE BIG SCREEN

To movie-star wanna-bes, being in the movies is the stuff dreams are made of. Right? Not quite. For a few people at the top, movie-making means limos, lights, and lots of extras. But wake up and smell the celluloid. Making movies is mostly hard work—just like any other profession. And the language of making movies is filled with lingo or jargon—just like any other profession. Some of our favorites are on the following pages.

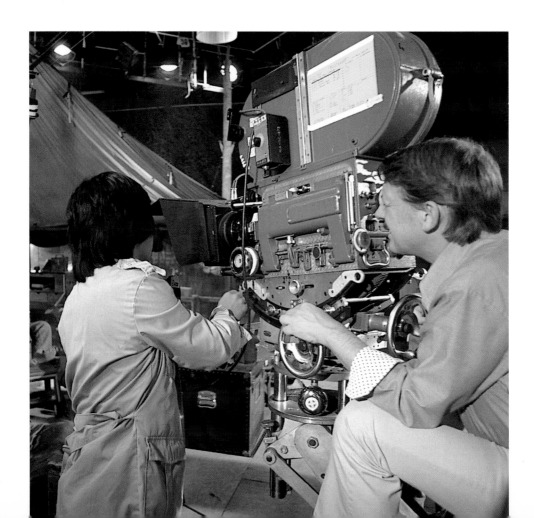

Best boy	The assistant chief lighting technician.
Cookie	Material with holes in it that creates a shadow pattern when it's placed over a camera lens.
Greenlight	Permission given to start a film project.
Horse	A support for rolls of film on the cutting table, where a movie is edited.
Pan	When a camera stays on a fixed point and moves horizontally across a scene.

Pitch   A writer may *pitch* a film idea to studio executives in the hope that they'll *greenlight* his or her project.

Rushes   Daily prints of a film that give the director and others a chance to see how work on the film is going.

Score	Music for a film that is usually recorded after the film has been edited.
Snake	A kind of cable wire used for filming.
Turtle	Large lights are mounted on a gadget that looks like a turtle.
Wrap	"It's a wrap" means that work on the film is complete for the day.

ON THE SMALLER SCREEN

If your home has a 41-inch TV, calling television a "small screen" may seem kind of funny. You can giggle now, but there was a time when that's how people referred to television. Just as movie people have a language of their own, so do TV people. Here are some of the inside words that the networks use. Cover up the definitions on the right and try to guess what the terms mean. Then uncover them and see just how close you came.

Alligator   A metal spring clamp with rows of "teeth" that is used to attach lights and other items. Its edges look like the jaws of an alligator.

Antenna farm The place where the transmitting antennas for most or all of the TV stations in an area are located.

Birding The transmission or sending of radio and TV signals by way of satellite. To "lose the bird" is to have a transmission interrupted.

Bite A sound bite is a few, short, easy-to-understand lines that are taken from a taped speech or interview.

Bleeble A brief piece of music played between segments of a show.

Bump To cancel a guest or segment on a show.

Cough button A switch used by a radio announcer to turn off the microphone during a cough.

Cowcatcher A commercial before or at the beginning of a TV show. A real cowcatcher is a wedge on the front of a train engine that would clear the tracks. This cowcatcher clears the way for the program.

Crawl A breaking news bulletin or other message that scrolls across the bottom of a TV screen.

Dolly	A wheeled platform that carries a microphone or camera.
f/x or **fx**	Special effects
Gaffer	The head electrician
Green room	The room or waiting area where TV guests wait for their turn to go on the air.
Shaky cam	A film or TV segment made by a handheld camera. Why do you think it's called "shaky?"
Soap	A series that's usually run during the daytime. At one time these programs were sponsored mainly by soap companies.
Talking head	When a motionless person speaks right to the camera.
Zipper	The sound effect that signals a commercial is about to start.

This is an example of a talking head.

EVEN iF THE HEAD'S NOT iN THE GUTTER, iT'S A BAD BREAK

Once upon a time, *type* meant words and *printers* were people. How do you think books were set and words were put on the page before computers did the job? Type—the words on a page—was put in place, letter-by-letter, by people called printers. The type was said to be "hot" when it was being set by hand.

Journalism and publishing have always been professions with colorful lingo. Look at the following terms and then try to figure out what this chapter title means. Then try making up your own sentences using some of these terms.

Bad break	A line of text that ends or breaks at a bad point between words that should be together.
Bleed	A photo or artwork that extends to the edge of a page.
Crop	To cut out part of a photo so that it fits in a space.
Deck	Lines under the main headline that give more information.
Gutter	The inner margin of a printed page where the book folds.
Head	Short for headline, or title.

Morgue   An old-time word for a newspaper library.

Orphan   A word at the end of a paragraph that falls on a new page.

Scoop   A story that one newspaper covers before other papers get to it. To a reporter, getting a scoop is like hitting a grand slam home run.

Spine

Spine	The part of a bound book that connects the front and back covers.
Widow	A word at the end of a sentence that is on a line by itself.

So what does "Even if the head's not in the gutter, it's a bad break" mean? If you understand the lingo, it's easy. It means "The title is too long to print on one line without it spilling into the margin, and the place where it breaks onto the next line separates letters or words that should be together."

This is an example of a head that extends into the gutter.

Gutter

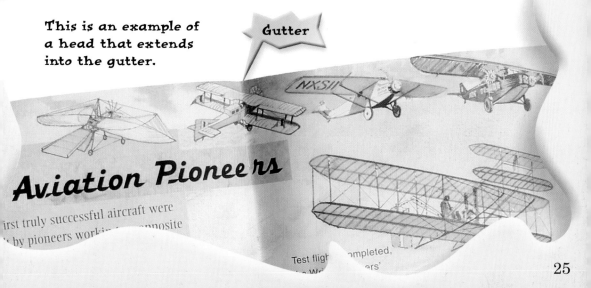

Aviation Pioneers

irst truly successful aircraft were
by pioneers work in   posite

Test flight   ompleted,

THAT'S THE SPIRIT!

If someone said, "A player caught a pass beyond the arc near the baseline and threw up a shot," what would you think it might mean? Could it mean that the player caught something nasty and got sick to his or her stomach? I doubt it. Would you even know that they were talking about basketball? Unless you're a total basketball fan, you might not. Basketball, like all sports, has its own jargon. So what did the person actually say? "The player caught the ball at the edge of the court outside the 3-point line and tried to toss it in." Piece of cake.

How are you at soccer terms? See how you do on this short quiz.

1. Bicycle kick

   a) when a player gets mad and kicks the opponent's bicycle

   b) an overhead kick that's also known as a
     scissors kick

2. Chip

a) a high pass over a player's head to a teammate

b) a snack to eat at half-time

3. Give-and-go

a) paying admission and getting into the game

b) when a player makes a short pass to a teammate and then receives the return pass

4. Trap

a) when a player uses any part of his or her body to bring the ball under control

b) when a group of teammates tries to get an opponent off the field

5. Wall

a) the goalpost

b) when a group of defenders stand shoulder-to-shoulder to defend a free kick, they build a human wall

Answers: 1. b, 2. a, 3. b, 4. a, 5. b

TAKE A HOIST TO TOP IT OFF

Like other professionals, construction workers and tradespeople have their own language. Here is some of their lingo:

Booming out Going where the work is, even if it's far from home.

Gang A crew working on a building. Big sites have about five gangs, each with a specific job. A raising gang unloads and erects steel beams. Bolter-upper gangs secure the beams with bolts.

Hoist	The elevator on a construction site.
Pusher	The foreman, or boss, on a job.
Shaping	Finding a new job.
Shanty	The wooden shack where the workers change into their work clothes.
Topping off	Finishing a job. It's a tradition to place an American flag on a building when it is topped off.

There are many more professions, and therefore, much more lingo to learn. We hope we've fired up your engines, at least a little bit.

So for now, that's a wrap. 10-4. Over and out.

And that, my friends, is lingo for . . . The End.

iNDEX

construction words
  booming out, 29
  gang, 29
  hoist, 30
  pusher, 30
  shaping, 30
  shanty, 30
  topping off, 30
jargon, 2
lingo, 2
movie words
  best boy, 15
  cookie, 15
  greenlight, 15
  horse, 15
  pan, 15
  pitch, 16
  rushes, 16
  score, 17
  snake, 17
  turtle, 17
  wrap, 17
pizza quiz, 11
pizza words
  destroy it, 11
  flyers, 12
  fungus, 12
  green slime, 12

screamers, 13
printing words
  bad break, 23
  bleed, 23
  crop, 23
  deck, 23
  gutter, 23
  head, 23
  morgue, 24
  orphan, 24
  printer, 22
  scoop, 24
  spine, 25
  type, 22
  widow, 25
soccer quiz, 26
sports words
  bicycle kick, 26
  chip, 27
  give-and-go, 27
  trap, 27
  wall, 28
television words
  alligator, 18
  antenna farm, 19
  birding, 19
  bite, 19
  bleeble, 20

bump, 20
cough button, 20
cowcatcher, 20
crawl, 20
dolly, 21
fx or f/x, 21
gaffer, 21
green room, 21
shaky cam, 21
soap, 21
talking head, 21
zipper, 21
weather words
  chase hotel, 3
  chocolate gale, 4
  chocolatero, 4
  dog days, 5
  dustbusting, 6
  fogeater, 8
  forecaster, 3
  lamb blast, 7
  little brother/
  little sister, 7
  snoweater, 8
  socked in, 9
  storm chaser, 3
  white elephant, 3
  wind sock, 9